THE SOURCES OF THE STORIES

There are many versions of the fairy tales told in this book.
The storytellers listed below wrote, or wrote down, the best-
known versions, on which the present tellings are based.
The date is the original year of publication.

Hansel and Gretel · Jacob and Wilhelm Grimm 1812
The Gingerbread Man · Sara Cone Bryant 1907
The Six Swans · Jacob and Wilhelm Grimm 1812

This 1986 edition is published by Derrydale Books, distributed by
Crown Publishers, Inc., by arrangement with Walker Books Limited.
Manufactured in Italy

Library of Congress Cataloging in Publication Data
Hayes, Sarah.
Hansel and Gretel; The gingerbread man; The
six swans.

(Read me a story)
Summary: Retellings of three well-known tales.
1. Fairy tales. [1. Fairy tales. 2. Folklore]
I. Hadley, Colin, ill. II. Title. III. Series:
Hayes, Sarah. Read me a story.
PZ8.H333Han   1986   398.2'1'0943 [E]   86-6404
ISBN 0-517-61549-5

h g f e d c b a

HANSEL AND GRETEL

THE GINGERBREAD MAN

THE SIX SWANS

Retold by Sarah Hayes

Illustrated by Colin Hadley

DERRYDALE BOOKS
NEW YORK

HANSEL AND GRETEL

Once upon a time two children called Hansel and Gretel lived in the forest with their father and stepmother. Their father was a woodcutter, and he was always poor. But one winter he became poorer than ever.

'We cannot even feed Hansel and Gretel properly,' he said to his wife one night.

'Why bother to feed them when we can't feed ourselves?' said his wife. 'We could leave them in the forest. They would never find the way back.'

The woodcutter was horrified by this idea, but his wife was cruel and strong-willed and eventually he was forced to agree. Fortunately hunger had kept Hansel and Gretel awake and they had overheard their parents talking.

'Do not worry, Sister,' said Hansel.
'I have a plan.' He slipped out of the house
and gathered a pocketful of white pebbles.

In the morning the woodcutter and his wife
gave the children a crust of bread and took
them into the forest. Every so often Hansel
stopped and looked back at the house.

'What can you see, boy?' asked his
stepmother.

'I can see my little white cat on the roof,
Mother,' replied Hansel.

'Nonsense,' snapped the stepmother. 'All
you can see is sunshine on the chimney-pot.'
But Hansel saw neither cat nor chimney-pot,
for he had only turned around to throw down
a pebble from his pocket.

Soon they were deep in the forest. The
woodcutter built a fire and told the children to
wait while he and his wife went away to chop
wood. Hansel and Gretel waited and waited
but no one came back. Night fell and wolves
began to howl.

'Do not be afraid, Sister,' said Hansel. 'The moon will be out soon and we will find our way home.' When the moon rose, the white pebbles gleamed like silver coins and guided the children back to their house.

The woodcutter was amazed and overjoyed when the children returned, but his wife was furious. She had failed once to get rid of the children but she would not fail again.

In the morning, for the second time, the woodcutter and his wife led the children deep into the forest. Hansel stopped every so often to look back at the house.

'What can you see, boy?' asked his stepmother.

'I can see my little white pigeon on the roof, Mother,' said Hansel.

'Nonsense,' snapped his stepmother. 'All you can see is sunshine on the chimney-pot.'

But Hansel saw neither pigeon nor chimney-pot, for he had only turned around to drop crumbs from the crust his father had given him.

Again the children were left to wait by the fire, and again the wolves began to howl as night fell. But when the moon rose, no crumbs gleamed to guide the children home, for birds had eaten them.

For two days Hansel and Gretel wandered in the forest looking for the way home. There were only berries to eat, and at night they sheltered wherever they could, hoping the

wolves would not find them. On the third day, weak with hunger, they saw a beautiful snow-white bird and followed it. As they stumbled into a clearing, they saw in front of them a house made of gingerbread. The roof was sponge cake, the chimneys were twisted sugar canes, and the windows were made of sugar baked as clear as glass.

Hansel rushed forward and broke off a piece of the roof. As he ate it a little voice sang out:

'*Nibble, nibble, little mouse,*
Who's that nibbling at my house?'

Hansel answered:

'*Do not fear, no mouse is near.*
It is only the wind in the trees you hear.'

He broke off another piece of the roof while Gretel pulled out a windowpane and started eating it.

Just then the door of the little house opened and out came an old woman. She smiled at the children and beckoned to them. 'Come in, come in, little mice,' she said. 'Stay with me for awhile. I have good food to eat and comfortable beds for you to sleep in.' Hansel and Gretel were happy to go inside, and after they had eaten they fell into bed and went straight to sleep.

The old woman crept upstairs to look at the sleeping children. She touched Hansel's rosy cheek. 'Yes, I shall have that one first,' she said and cackled softly, for she was really a horrible witch who lured little children to her house and ate them.

In the morning the witch locked Hansel in
a cage and ordered Gretel to cook him a meal.
'We must fatten that one up,' she said, so Hansel
dined like a king while Gretel ate only scraps.

Every day the witch went to the cage and asked Hansel to put out a finger so she could feel how fat he was getting. She was very short-sighted, and every day Hansel put out a little bone for her to feel. After a month the witch grew impatient. 'Fat or not, that one is for the pot,' she said and ordered Gretel to build a fire for the oven. Then she asked Gretel to climb into the oven to see if it was hot. Gretel saw that the witch meant to slam the

door and roast her at the same time as her brother, so she pretended not to understand.

'But how do I open the door?' she asked.

'Like this,' said the witch, and showed her.

'But how do I climb in?' asked Gretel.

'Climb in like this,' said the witch, and she crawled into the oven. At once Gretel slammed the door and the witch was burned to death.

'The witch is dead, the witch is dead, the wicked witch is dead!' sang Gretel, and she ran to release Hansel from the cage. The children snatched up a bag of the witch's gold and ran away from the house as fast as they could.

Before long they had run right through the forest and back home.

The woodcutter cried with joy when he saw them, and his wife could say nothing at all – for she was dead and buried long since, which was good enough for her.

THE GINGERBREAD MAN

Once upon a time a little old man and a little old woman lived together in a little old house. They longed to have children, so one day the little old woman made herself a gingerbread man. She cut out the dough and put in two raisins for eyes and four raisins down the front for buttons. Then she put the gingerbread man in the oven to bake.

While the little old woman's back was turned, the oven door flew open and out hopped the gingerbread man. He ran out of the house, down the front path and through the gate. The little old man and the little old woman ran after him shouting, 'Stop! Stop!'

But they could not catch the gingerbread man,
who laughed and shouted:

'Run, run as fast as you can,
You can't catch me,
I'm the gingerbread man.'

The gingerbread man ran and ran, and soon
he passed a field where a farmer was cutting hay.
The farmer ran after him shouting, 'Stop! Stop!
I want to eat you.' But he could not catch the
gingerbread man, who laughed and shouted:

'I've outrun an old woman
And an old man,
And I can run away from you,
I can, I can.
Run, run as fast as you can,
You can't catch me,
I'm the gingerbread man.'

The gingerbread man ran and ran, and soon
he passed a cow munching grass. The cow ran
after him shouting, 'Stop! Stop! I want to eat
you.' But she could not catch the gingerbread
man, who laughed and shouted:

'I've outrun an old woman
And an old man,
And a farmer cutting hay,
And I can run away from you,
    I can, I can.
Run, run as fast as you can,
You can't catch me,
    I'm the gingerbread man.'

The gingerbread man ran and ran, and soon he passed a bear up a tree. The bear shouted, 'Stop! Stop! I want to eat you.' He climbed down and ran after him, but he could not catch the gingerbread man, who laughed and shouted:

'I've outrun an old woman
And an old man,
And a farmer cutting hay,
And a cow munching grass,
And I can run away from you,
    I can, I can.
Run, run as fast as you can,
You can't catch me,
    I'm the gingerbread man.'

The gingerbread man ran and ran, and soon
he passed a fox in a meadow. The fox thought
the gingerbread man would make a fine meal.
'Stop! Stop!' he cried and ran after him, but
the gingerbread man ran even faster shouting:

'I've outrun an old woman
And an old man,
And a farmer cutting hay,
And a cow munching grass,
And a bear up a tree,
And I can run away from you,
*   I can, I can.'*

'Of course you can,' said the wily fox. 'I
don't want to catch you anyhow.'

Just then the gingerbread man came to a
river. 'Jump on my tail,' said the fox. 'I'd
be happy to carry you across.' So the
gingerbread man jumped on the fox's tail.

But the water was deep and soon the fox said, 'You are too heavy for my tail and we shall sink. Jump on my back.'

So the gingerbread man jumped on the fox's back.

But the water was deep and soon the fox said, 'You are too heavy for my back and we shall sink. Jump on my head.'

So the gingerbread man jumped on the fox's head.

But the water was deep and soon the fox said, 'You are too heavy for my head and we shall sink. Jump on my nose.'

So the gingerbread man jumped on the fox's nose.

As soon as he reached the bank, the fox opened
his mouth and crunched him up – snip, snap.
And that was the end of the gingerbread man.

THE SIX SWANS

There was once a king who lost his way in the forest and feared he would die if he did not find a way out before nightfall. He was about to give up hope when an old woman appeared. 'I will show you the path if you marry my daughter,' she said. As the king's first wife was dead and the old woman's daughter was very beautiful, the king agreed. But when he arrived home with his new wife, he discovered his mistake. The old woman was a witch, and the new queen had inherited all her mother's evil ways.

The king already had seven children – six sons and a daughter who bore a golden star on her forehead.

Fearing that the witch-queen might do them some harm, he ordered his servants to hide the children in the forest. When he wished to visit them, he took out a magic ball of wool which unrolled and led him to the children's hiding place.

Soon the king was spending nearly all his time with the children and the witch-queen became suspicious. One day she stole the ball of wool and found the way to the children's house. The boys thought their father had arrived and ran forward to meet him. But as they did so, the witch-queen grabbed them and pulled magic shirts over their heads. Into each shirt she had woven a wicked spell which turned the princes into swans. The great birds struggled and flapped in her arms and then flew off. When there were six swans in the sky, the witch-queen went away.

A little later the princess with the golden star came out of the house to call her brothers for supper. She called and called, but no one came. For three days she wandered in the forest, calling and searching. On the evening of the third day she came to a little hut on the far side of the forest. As she sat down to rest she heard the beating of wings, and six swans flew through the window and landed in front of her. In a moment the six princes had stripped off their swanskins and now stood before their sister.

'We cannot stay princes for long,' they told her. 'For fifteen minutes every day we regain our rightful shape, and then we must turn back into swans.'

'How can I break this dreadful spell?' asked the princess.

'It is too much to ask,' said the brothers.

'Ask it,' implored the princess, and her brothers told her what she had to do.

'For six years you must never speak, and each year you must weave a shirt of star-

flowers, one for each of us.'

'That is not too much to ask,' said the princess quietly.

The princes turned back into swans and flew away.

For a year the princess searched for star-flowers. She found just enough to make one shirt. The leaves hurt her hands as she sewed, but she never made a sound.

In two years she had made two shirts. Toward the end of the third year a young king who was out hunting saw the princess hiding in a tree.

'Come down!' he cried, but the princess said nothing and threw down her gold necklace.

'Come down!' he cried again. Still the princess said nothing and threw down her golden belt. Then the king sent his huntsman up to fetch her. Never a word did she speak, but the king fell in love with her all the same and brought her to his palace to be queen.

Now the king's mother was jealous of the young queen with the golden star on her forehead. When a princess was born, the king's mother stole away the baby and said that the star-queen had killed it. The king was angry with his mother and said that his star-queen was too gentle ever to have done such a horrible deed.

When a second child was born, the king's mother again stole away the baby and blamed the young queen.

Again the king was angry with his mother. He knew that his star-queen was innocent and would prove it if only she could speak.

When a third child was born, the king's mother again stole away the baby. This time she put a drop of blood on the star-queen's dress and the king was made to believe that his wife really had killed the baby. 'She will be burned alive,' he said. And still the star-queen never said a word.

By now six years had almost passed. Five shirts of star-flowers had been made, and as the fire was being built the young queen sewed and sewed at the sixth. Soon she had finished it, except for one sleeve.

The star-queen was brought out and the fire
was lit. The flames began to crackle and rise
high in the air. Then a beating of wings
was heard and six swans flew out of the
forest. As they swooped down to untie
the queen, she threw a star-flower
shirt over each of their heads.
Instantly six princes stood
before the king. But in
place of an arm, the
youngest prince
had the great
white wing
of a swan.

At last the star-queen could speak, and she told the king of her brothers' enchantment and of the lies his mother had told. The king soon found out where his mother had hidden the three children, and then he ordered her to be put on the fire and burned to ashes.

As for the star-queen, she lived happily with her husband, her children and her six brothers until the end of her days.